The Nutcracker in Harlem

By T. E. McMorrow   Illustrated by James Ransome

HARPER
An Imprint of HarperCollinsPublishers

ISBN 978-0-06-117598-5 (trade bdg.) — ISBN 978-0-06-117599-2 (lib. bdg.)

The artist used watercolors to create the illustrations for this book.
Typography by Whitney Manger
17 18 19 20 21 SCP 10 9 8 7 6 5 4 3 2 1
❖
First Edition

To my wife and partner, Carole, whose inspiration
and support made this book possible.
—T.E.M.

For my wife, Lesa.
—J.R.

It was snowing in Harlem on Christmas Eve.

The party at Marie's house swirled with colors, gold and red and green. Mama and Poppy were dancing. Miss Addie sang, and Uncle Cab played the piano.

Marie loved the sound of Christmas.

"Join in, Marie," Uncle Cab called out.

Marie looked down. She wished she could sing, but Marie was afraid she wasn't any good. Certainly not like Miss Addie or Uncle Cab.

The song ended. It was time for gifts!

Every year, Uncle Cab would give Marie a doll and Freddie some toy soldiers. They were carved from a magical wood, Uncle Cab always said.

He handed Freddie his gift.

"And now for my Marie," said Uncle Cab.

"A nutcracker," said Marie. "A drummer boy nutcracker!"

Dum diddy dum dum, dum-dee-dum, played the nutcracker on his drum.

Uncle Cab sang a tune to the beat of the little drummer. The room again filled with song.

Everyone in the house was singing or dancing. Everyone except Marie.

Miss Addie knelt next to Marie. "Will you sing with me, Marie?" she asked.

Marie shook her head.

"Maybe next time," Miss Addie said. "Music lives inside everyone. You just have to let it out."

After dinner, Marie took the nutcracker and a slice of sweet potato pie and sat by the Christmas tree. The lights were soft and twinkling. She lay down, closed her eyes, and fell asleep.

Marie opened her eyes. The house had gone silent.

Outside, it had stopped snowing. A full moon glowed in the sky, and the living room was filled with a ghostly white light.

A rustling sound came
from the top of the tree, where
Mama had hung her favorite
ornaments, the glass birds.

It was almost as if the blue
glass bird was moving.

It was! The bird fluttered its
wings and began to sing. Then
the gold bird joined in, and the
red one, and the green one, too.

As the birds sang, the Christmas tree began to grow. It grew bigger and bigger until it towered over Marie. The ornaments, the presents, the dolls, and the soldiers grew, too.

Dum diddy dum dum, dum-dee-dum.

The nutcracker played his drum. The toy soldiers and dolls danced around the tree as the birds sang on.

Crash! The music stopped.

"Candy canes!" a voice squeaked.

Marie turned. A mouse army, all in uniform, was marching toward the tree.

A mouse general was leading them, his chest covered with shiny medals. "Candy canes!" he repeated. "Marzipan and chocolate! Charge!"

The nutcracker began to drum. *Dum-diddy-dum*!

The toy soldiers lined up behind him. They marched toward the mouse army.

One mouse turned and ran away. Then the entire army followed, all except the general.

"I want sweet potato pie!" the general shouted. He ran, jumped, and knocked the nutcracker down.

The drum fell to the ground.

When the drumming stopped, so did the toy soldiers. The mouse army advanced again.

"Charge!" the mouse general commanded.

What could Marie do?

She picked up the drum and put the strap over her neck.

Dum-diddy-dum!

The mouse army stopped, turned, and ran away.

The general glared but Marie kept drumming until he, too, fled.

As the mice ran, they began to shrink, getting smaller and smaller. The toy soldiers chased the mice through a hole in the wall and into the snow outside.

The glass birds sang as the soldiers returned. Marie joined the nutcracker in a dance. They swirled around and around. They seemed to be on a cloud. It started to snow, but it wasn't cold. Marie closed her eyes and began to sing.

"Marie?"
She opened her eyes.
It was morning.
"Did I miss Christmas?" Marie asked.
"Of course not, darling," Mama said.

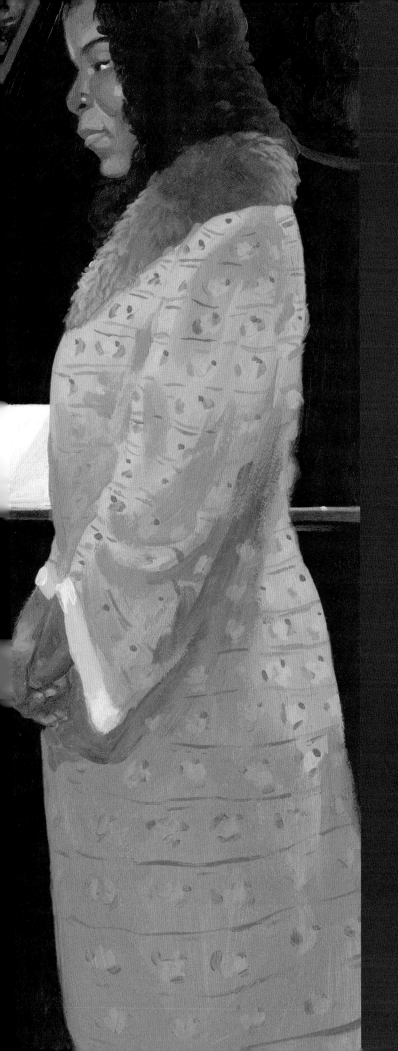

Under the tree were Marie's dolls, the
nutcracker, and something else: a drum.
She picked up the drumsticks.
Dum diddy dum dum, dum-dee-dum.
"Very good!" said Uncle Cab. He
began to sing a Christmas song. Momma
and Poppy and Miss Addie all joined in.
And so did Marie.

Author's Note

Years ago, I was hired as a stagehand for the Dance Theatre of Harlem, a ballet company and dance school based in the Sugar Hill neighborhood of Harlem in New York City. I watched the performers rehearse long hours, exploring the happy and sad moments of life through music and dance. Those memories have stayed with me to this day.

When my wife suggested I write a retelling of her favorite Christmas story, "The Nutcracker and the Mouse King" by E. T. A. Hoffmann, it seemed natural for me to set my retelling in Sugar Hill. After all, Hoffmann's classic is best known as told through Tchaikovsky's famous ballet *The Nutcracker*. I wanted my version of the story to be set in the place where I had seen the power of music and dance transform people, performers, and audiences alike.

As I researched Sugar Hill, I focused on a famous period near the beginning of the twentieth century, when Harlem attracted a growing number of artists and intellectuals. In the 1920s, when our story is set, the thriving local culture became known as the Harlem Renaissance.

The music of that period in particular had a major impact on American culture. Jazz was a combination of African rhythm and European harmony. It allowed musicians to find the story within the music, to express themselves freely in ways that hadn't been possible before.

Two of the fictional characters in this book are named after musicians based in Harlem in that era. Miss Addie is a nod to Adelaide Hall, a vocalist with Duke Ellington's band. Uncle Cab is a tribute to Cab Calloway, a singer and bandleader. Both Hall and Calloway had unique vocal styles and were extremely influential on the way jazz and popular music evolved in America. Just as the memory of the Nutcracker remained with Marie, so too did the memory of the Harlem Renaissance remain in the American soul.

—T. E. M.